# GIRL UNDER

## WRITTEN BY

### HEIDI LOUISE WILLIAMS

Gem-in-Eye Publishing

All rights reserved: No part of this publication may be transmitted or reproduced by any means, electronic, mechanical, photocopying or otherwise without prior permission of the publisher.

First published 2021
Gem-in-Eye Publishing

GIRL UNDER THE FLOOR

Text copyright © 2021 Heidi Louise Williams
Cover image © Heidi Louise Williams
Graphic designer for cover image:
Antonio Lorenzo (MDM Publicidad, Nerja)

ISBN 9781999378325

All Characters and events in this book, other than those clearly in the public domain, are fictitious and any resemblance to real persons, being alive or dead is purely coincidental.

DEDICATED TO

ALL MY LONG TERM

LONG DISTANCE FRIENDS

WHO I SEE SELDOM

BUT THINK OF OFTEN

# CHAPTER ONE

In January of 1960, Charles Rose made certain renovations to the eighty-five-year-old one story country house on Culloden Hill Drive for unconventional reasons.

He removed the kitchen units from the room at the back that faced the small garden, leaving only the sink and a few shelves. He turned that back room into the bedroom. The master bedroom that had been at the front of the house was transformed into the new kitchen.

He had a very specific reason for wanting his bedroom at the back of the house. It was to do with what was in the floor. Having the kitchen at the front also meant he could keep an eye on the passing of the nosy neighbourhood.

Under the floor in the old kitchen, there was a long box where in the old days, when they didn't have fridges, they would keep the fruits and vegetables in a built-in larder box in the cool crawl space under the house. When Charles' grandfather had built the house in 1875, he had secured a coffin length box in the floor; giving his wife plenty of storage and also a coffin to bury him in if he passed first, to save her money. He was a practical man was Charles Rose's grandfather, David Charles Rose.

He did not pass first, and he carved his wife of fifty years a more fitting and beautiful coffin from red cedar wood.

Since having refrigerators, the box was no longer used and lay forgotten under the kitchen floor. His oldest and youngest children had long forgotten about the box, except the middle child, Philip. Philip never forgot about the box but his father was not buried in it.

Philip was fated to always remember the box. Their mother treated him differently from his siblings. She said he always sought out trouble so he needed more discipline. On occasions when he had stolen from the larder or answered her back, she cleared everything out, and made him lie in the coffin box under the floor. She closed the two lids for twenty minutes.

Philip's grandfather had split the lid of the box in the middle to form two doors, so that his wife didn't have to lift such a long door - and it would keep some of the cool air in each time his wife needed to get something. There was a wooden eye in the middle plank where the patterns flowed like veins around the notch in the plank. The eye had a chip out of the corner that Philip could breathe through. He would press his eye against the little hole, and try to see his brother and sister eating at the kitchen table.

The twenty minutes would seem like an eternity, lying there unable to move, people walking about on the top of his coffin.

Eventually, his mother would unlocked the doors, let him up, give him a spanking, and send him to bed.

When his parents died, Philip moved back into the house with Nancy, his pregnant wife.

It had always been a difficult marriage. Philip was strict, domineering and very jealous. He controlled his timid wife, completely. At the same time that Nancy fell pregnant, Philip had been made unemployed, and so it was a blessing that his childhood house had become available two months prior.

Nancy was innocent of most things, being twelve years younger than Philip. She had been spoilt by her parents and didn't know how to cook or clean properly. To make her learn to be a more dutiful spouse, Philip would lock his claustrophobic young wife in the coffin like box.

At first she would scream and scratch and claw at the box trying to get out, but when the children were home, she laid still and quiet to not upset them.

The hole in the wooden eye had started off small, just a corner missing but Nancy had frantically picked at it to make it bigger so that she had more air to breathe, and eventually the whole wooden eye popped out leaving a perfectly round two centimetre circle in the plank, which always amazed Philip Rose how perfectly smooth and circular it was.

Nancy learnt to escape those times of panic with astral levitation. Not that she knew anything about astral levitation but she escaped into fantasies of travelling to faraway places and eventually her spirit drifted out of her body.

At first, Philip would lock his wife in the box for only a day or two, but over the years it got worse. For almost the entire year that Charlie was five, his mother was just an eyeball poking out of the middle of the kitchen floor.

# CHAPTER TWO

His mother sneezed as Charlie walked over her.

'Bless you, Mama,' Charlie said to the hole in the floor. The eyeball appeared which he could never quite get used to; it still scared him a little.

'Is that you, Charlie?' came Mama's voice between the boards.

'Yes Mama. It's me, Charlie,' he said kneeling down beside the eyeball in the hole. 'Is that you, Mama?'

'Are you okay, Charlie?' Mama asked concerned.

'Yes. Are you okay, Mama?'

'Could you get me some water please, Charlie,' his mother replied.

'Stop talking to that wretched woman! Get your glass of water, Charlie, and get back here and eat your dinner!' Charlie's father demanded from the table in the living room, where he and Charlie's siblings were waiting. They no longer ate meals in the kitchen. It was uncomfortable for the children to have the eyeball in the floor watching them eat.

Philip had thought about making the hole smaller again, sealing most of it up, but his wife was quieter now and so the children were quieter and able to ignore her.

Charlie pushed the stool to the sink and climbed up. He turned on the tap and let it run until it was cold. He filled his glass - carefully put it on the side - climbed down - pushed the stool back against the wall, and then reached up to get his glass.

He kneeled by the hole.

'Here, Mama, here's some water for you,' he said sympathetically, tipping his glass.

'Only pour a little slowl...' she tried to tell him but the water came gushing down onto her face. She moved her mouth to below to the hole. Charlie could hear her spluttering and choking so he stopped.

'GET BACK TO THE TABLE!' his father yelled, coming into the kitchen, grabbing him by the collar and dragging him back to his cheese sandwich. His father wasn't much of a chef.

In the middle of the night, Charlie would sneak out of bed to feed Mama morsels of food through the hole in the floor.

After eating, Mama would sing little Charlie lullabies through the hole in the floor, and tell him that she loved him, and that everything would be okay. She would poke a finger out through the hole, and Charlie would stroke it, lovingly. This is what he came to relate to as a mother, a woman in parts – a finger, an eyeball, lips, breathe from an invisible being below.

Charlie missed having a mother more than his siblings. Sometimes during the night, when his father was sound asleep and Charlie sat talking to the eyeball in the floor, Charlie would carve at the wood below the hole with his fingernail trying to expand the hole so that he could see more of his mother but the wood was too hard and he was too small and could produce nothing but scratches in the form of a lock that he dreamed he could open to release his mother.

The children were forbidden to mention their mother ever. They were not allowed to talk to her or even acknowledge that she was there or there would be beatings.

Philip Rose had been raised with the Bible, and he made his three children learn all the scriptures. It kept them busy and out of trouble, and he could make them recite scriptures if the social services came sniffing around, to show them that the children were going to school, church, and Sunday school. They hardly went to any of those institutions as they had to keep the house clean and do all of Mama's chores now that she was living dead.

Philip always excused his wife's absence on those rare occasions the social services came snooping, telling the social that she was temporarily staying with a sick friend or at work. The children would repeat what they had been taught to say.

Harry who was two years older than Charlie, and Judy who was eleven months younger than Philip, never spoke to their mother. They believed their fathers words which he twisted from the holy book that showed she was wicked, an adulterous, a lazy wife and a bad mother.

The older and the younger child eventually ignored the eyeball in the floor. Trying not to tread on it was the only acknowledgment they gave to their mother. Eventually, they learnt to walk around the outskirts of the room so they would have to pay her no heed.

The cut long rectangle in the floorboards, which served as the lid to the shallow coffin below, could be opened in two parts. Both parts had locks, and only Philip Rose had the key.

He would open the sides alternately depending on whether he remembered to feed his wife or if he just wanted to have sex with her. For the later, he would unlock only the second half of the box. There was no reason for him to see her uncomfortable screams.

Charlie couldn't see his mother's screams either but from his tiny bedroom he could hear them. He wished Mama didn't make so much noise. It bothered him, made him angry.

As Charlie grew up, these things became more normal to him. His ears toned out the horrific sounds until he couldn't hear Mama's screams anymore, or her nails scratching at the wood all through the night. He blocked the bad sounds out - but he heard the silence, the night the night the eerie sounds stopped.

He knew instinctively that his Mama was dead.

# CHAPTER THREE

Charlie Rose ran his hand along the hanging rugs on the stand in the corner of the department store. Something fluffy maybe? Something that wouldn't move a lot or be easy to slip on. Maybe he should buy something in the colour that went with the room to make it look more natural; to make it look like it was added to match the room, an accessory. Not there to cover something up. Not an accessory to murder or anything suspicious looking. White? To match the walls? White is the colour of innocence. Subconsciously, would it deter anyone from looking under it? Who would look? He had no friends, hadn't spoken to his brother or his sister in years, his father was dead after suffering a heart attack, and his mother, according to their father, had run off with the milkman to Barbados never to be heard from again. Charlie had always known that this story was a lie and that his mother was dead but because he was terrified of his father Charlie kept quiet.

Charles Rose assured himself that no one would go in his room unless he was there too, but if in the worst case scenario: a snooping policeman on the off chance made a wrong turn looking for the bathroom; would a white rug subconsciously seem innocent?

Long or short? Long might give the subconscious suspicion that something long like a body was hidden under there.

He decided on a short white fluffy rug with anti-slip tracking on the back. He also bought cable ties in red, duct tape in silver, and four large non-scrape round patches to stick on the feet of the bed to stop the scraping on the wooden floor each time he moved it.

He paid in cash. Charles Rose watched the girl as she swiped the items and totalled them. He concluded that she had overly large shoulders. She probably wouldn't fit. She had dark hair but her eyes were wrong – they were brown, not blue. She smiled, noticing him looking at her. He looked down at his wallet without a return smile, took out the exact money, collected his purchases and left.

On the way home, he saw a teenage girl, fifteen or sixteen who would fit perfectly into the box. She had darkish hair but he couldn't see her eyes. He tailed her for a while. She stopped to light a cigarette, and he drove off. She would be too high maintenance because she smoked; probably had bad teeth. Really it was her hair. It wasn't quite dark enough.

He caught sight of himself in the wing mirror as he pulled away. He looked away quickly. He had never liked his reflection since his father had split his upper lip with his ring when Charlie had been up past his bedtime.

His mother had to stitch it quickly when her husband went to buy milk, as Philip Rose refused to let his son visit the hospital. He was a Jehovah's Witness like his daddy, and they believed what life delivered was part of the Lord's plan to make them stronger. So no one in the family went to doctors or dentists; God forbid shrinks.

It took nine crude stitches that left him with a four centimetre scar through his upper lip almost into his nose. Strangers always presumed that he had been born with an orofacial cleft.


When Charles Rose got home from the department store, he straight away put the stickers on the bottom of the feet of the bed that curled inwards like the paws of a great lion blended into the ornate mahogany wood of the grandiose bed. The short fluffy, innocent looking, white rug was placed temporarily over the hole. This fluffy rug did not cover all cut lines around the length of the lids of the box in the wooden floor but the cuts in the wood blended into the lines between the planks, and no one would notice them. Even knowing the two doors were there, without the two locks to direct you with the known distance three centimetres below, it would be still be hard to find where to open the box in the floor. Once unlocked, a butter knife would be required to slip down into the gap between the floorboards, to prize open the lid.

Charles Rose kept the butter knife in the top drawer beside the heavy wooden antique queen bed that his grandmother had died in.

The key that unlocked the two doors to the lid of the box was kept in the bottom drawer.

Charles Rose went to make a cup of tea. He stood at the kitchen window, staring out across the green to where the older teenagers collected and hung out on the benches between the trees at the back of the playground.

He watched them unseen from the kitchen.

If anyone walking on the pavement outside his house or passing in a car happened to look in, he was just busy doing the washing up or preparing food. It was normal to spend a long time every day by the kitchen window.

That afternoon, the perfect girl caught his eye. She looked so much like a young version of his mother. She was about seventeen, eighteen at the most. She was slim not skinny but small enough to fit.

Charles Rose looked through his expensive binoculars to see if the girl had the same eye colour as his mother. Mother had had very dark brown hair which made her blue eyes really stand out. With his high powered lenses, he could zoom in close enough to see her eyes were pale, but if they were blue he could not tell for sure. She was leaving the park. In panic, Charles Rose put down the binoculars and grabbed his coat and car keys.

# CHAPTER FOUR

'Excuse me. Have you seen an old woman in a nightdress running around on the loose? I've lost my mum and she has memory problems. She did this last week too! I found her close to here. She was completely disorientated and crying because she was so scared. I'm really worried about her,' Charles Rose said through the open window to the dark haired girl walking down the empty street.

'No, sorry! Haven't seen her! I hope you find her,' the girl replied, still keeping some distance away from the car but she was more relaxed as it was just some harmless guy who was just looking for his poor old mum. As he continued speaking, she came closer so as not to appear rude and to fully hear what he was saying.

'The only problem is she forgets who I am until I show her the photographs of her and the family.  When I initially approach her, she gets scared because she has had such a bad history with men. She gets confused and thinks that I am her dad. Women are able to keep her calm. It is always easier if a woman tells her she is okay and that I am her son, Charlie, come to take her home.  She just needs to know she is safe and that I'm her son, then she will be fine...Shit, was that her?' he said, faking that he had seen someone further down the road taking a left. The girl had been facing the car.

'That was her! I can't lose her! Please come with me. You can calm her until I show her the photos, and explain to her who she is, and then

I can get her in the car and take her home. Please! She hasn't eaten. She needs her medication. Quickly, I can't lose her! It is really dangerous for her to be out,' Charles Rose pleaded in urgency. The girl hesitated only a second but the woman needed her help right now, too urgent to really think about it, so she got into the car.

'Where did you see her go?' Taylor Mason asked, closing the car door, silently praying that this guy was trustworthy.

'She went down that road on the left,' Charlie Rose replied, starting the car back up.

When they came up on the left street, the dark-haired girl in the passenger seat predictably turned her head away and looked to the left. Charles Rose slid the needle into her neck and injected the sedative before her hand reached up to swipe away what had bitten her.

His hard fist was clenched and ready to knock her out before she had time to turn back to him.

# CHAPTER FIVE

Charles Rose dragged the heavy mahogany head of the bed ten centimetres away from the wall. This was so that the end legs would be one on each side of the box, keeping the lids down, extremely heavy, and impossible to lift up on either side.

The hole was now covered from view by the bed. The mat was put back three centimetres away from the hole, no longer covering it, so that oxygen could keep this unusual type of stored goods fresh.

The mat still covered the locks so no one passing in the hall or standing in the room could look across the bed and see them in the floor at its feet.

Taylor Mason woke up thinking she was in a bad dream. She tried to sit up in the darkness but only lifted her neck before her face was pressed against what felt like wooden planks.

Had her hands been free, she would have had enough room to squeeze her arms down beside her but there was not an inch to spare in width.

Her hands and feet were bound with what felt like cable ties. There was a strip of duct tape over her mouth. She was naked except for her open flannel shirt that he had kept on her to protect her back against the bottom of the box. Someone must have cut her bra off, she thought to herself, or put her shirt back on again after taking it off.

He had indeed cut all her clothes off, except the shirt which he had unbuttoned while she had been unconscious.

There was a soft padded sheet under her bottom, to soak up her pee she presumed with a dreaded realisation that she wasn't getting out, even to go to the bathroom.

The lid of the box was about four centimetres above her nose. Her feet were pressed against the bottom of the box but there was space above her head and she could slide up and down about ten centimetres.

When she slid up to the top, her eye passed a hole. One hole of faint light. In paranoia, she pressed her nostril to it first and sucked in the air from above. Then she slid down a bit, and put her eye to the hole. There was dim light outside of the darkness. There was something large and dark suspended six centimetres above her, with low light coming in from the side below it through a curvy triangular shape in the darkness.

It was quiet. No sounds at all. She was trapped in silence, in darkness, unable to move. Was she dead?

No answers came for agonizing hours. Not until someone suddenly turned the lights on.

# CHAPTER SIX

When the lights went on outside her hole, Taylor instantly recognised that she was under the floor beneath a low set bed with a shaped wooden skirt around the sides. Taylor began muffled screaming and banging on the underneath of the lid with the heels of her joined hands.

The bed was dragged back and a creepy looking man in a grey raincoat appeared. He looked down at her, curiously. He had a flat nose and what appeared to be a cleft lip. He had really dark eyes, the whites of which were red. He had a greasy seventies side parting and smelt of Old Spice. He was monstrous in an unimpressive way.

Taylor Mason stared wide-eyed in terror at her captor and continued to make as much noise as she could.

'Be quiet! You have to learn to be quiet like a beautiful butterfly. If you are not beautiful in spirit like a butterfly you will never make a good mother, and then you must be punished for not doing your duty; for not being the best of you. The best you can be as a woman, as a wife. In the eyes of a vengeful god we cannot let you fail. We must be vengeful in his name. Leviticus states an "eye for an eye, tooth for a tooth. Just as another has received injury from him, so it will be given". You have been warned! Ecclesiastes 8:11 says, "When the sentence of a crime is not quickly carried out, people's hearts are filled with schemes to do wrong." For whoever touches you, touches the apple of his eye' he quoted, kneeing down, almost whispering into the hole at the end of his message. She looked up through the hole and he jabbed his finger in her eye. She squealed and tried to wriggle to the side in pain. With the butter knife at the ready, he quickly unlocked the top half of the box, opened the lid, and tore off the duct tape covering her mouth before she could open her eyes.

'Mother fucker!' was all she could manage to throw at him before the lid slammed shut on her face. She heard the key turn in the lock, and the bed pulled back over the hole.

He stood up and went to the bedroom sink to pour water into a disposable bottle that he'd washed up after drinking the blue sports drink he had purchased and drunk on the way home.

It had a nozzle to release the water slower in comfortable gulps.

He screwed the top back on, pushed the bed back against the wall, lifted the nozzle, and inserted it through the hole into her cage like a water bottle for a hamster. It dripped slowly onto her forehead. She slid up and placed her mouth to the tapering nozzle, and gratefully drank. She didn't care if it was drugged - all for the better, quite frankly. Considering the circumstances, that would have been a kindness.

When she could drink no more she tried to push the nozzle closed with her nose but she pushed the bottle upwards out of the hole and it rolled away. He picked it up and put it on the nightstand with the butter knife in the top drawer and the key in the bottom drawer

She heard him get undressed. She strained her eye to the side towards the light and saw his clothes get tossed to the floor. She heard him climb onto the bed.

For the next twenty minutes, she was subjected to him groaning, and the joints of the bed creaking against the old legs as he jerked himself off.

Then it went completely dark; for hours and hours and hours and hours...

# CHAPTER SEVEN

Men usually wake up with a hard-on. She was dreading the morning.

The light went on. The bed was pushed back, and a cylinder pillar of light hit her face. She positioned her eye into the hole so she could see what was coming.

'Now you have had time to cool off and become more comfortable in your new and permanent surroundings, this morning we can have some fun,' he said standing over her completely naked, unashamed of his scrawniness.

Taylor spat at him through the circular space. He knelt down beside the hole.

'Did you spit at me, you disgusting dirty whore? "Then shall his brother's wife come unto him in the presence of the elders, and loose his shoe, and spit in his face." Dirty, dirty butterfly!'

He coughed up mucus, snorted, and coughed up more, swished it around his mouth and dirty teeth, and then dribbled the brown, green and yellow liquid slowly from his mouth down through the hole. Unexpectedly, because she could not see him, it dribbled into her open mouth. She quickly closed her lips and turned her head to the side. It trailed thick and stringy across her cheek and dribbled down her neck. Almost puking, she spat and wiped her face with her shoulder. She could smell it on her shirt.

The lower lid of the box opened. It was nice for a second to feel the air on her skin. He cut the cable ties around her ankles, grabbed her legs as she kicked out, and then spread them.

She wriggled and cried out, tried to scratch him with her broken nails but she couldn't reach him with her hands bound and her upper torso trap under the other lid.

'You can move and struggle all you want. "Be fruitful and multiply and fill the earth and subdue it, and have dominion over the fish of the sea and over the birds of the heavens and over every living thing that moves on the earth." From now on, I will have dominion over you and all things that move,' he stated.

The cable ties had cut into her wrists and ankles. They stung when he grabbed her in those places but everything he did hurt her. She lay still. There was only one way to get away. She distracted her mind, and her consciousness floated out of her body while he raped her.

When it was over, he put an adult nappy on her, cable tied her ankles, and then locked up the lower lid.

For twenty minutes there was only darkness again. Then the upper lid opened, and he helped her to sit up. He served her breakfast. Handfed her a fried egg sandwich, cut into small squares, and he bought a glass to her mouth to let her take small gulps of freshly squeezed orange juice.

When she had eaten, he produced a bowl of water and a toothbrush. He squeezed paste onto the brush and aimed it at her mouth. Submissively, she opened up. He was thorough. The mounting foam choked her and poured down her chin. He wiped her face with a cloth, gave her a swig of water and told her to spit it back into the bowl. He wiped her face again, and told her to lie down.

'I need to go to the bathroom, please,' Taylor pleaded.

'No!' he replied, slamming the lid shut and locking it.

Taylor cried as she relieved herself into the nappy. It felt warming but within fifteen minutes it started to itch. He didn't replace it until lunchtime.

Having only opened the bottom half of the box, he ripped open the sticky strips on the sides, and pulled off the urine soaked nappy. He washed her with a flannel and a bowl of warm water from the tap. He tenderly dried her, smeared a white anti-rash cream over her private parts, and put her into a fresh nappy. He did not touch her sexually. He applied the cream like a parent would a child, and Taylor was grateful, until he said something twisted.

'There you go, Mama, all nice and clean, like you used to do to me.'

Taylor didn't say anything but she felt scared. How sick in the head was this guy? He closed the lower lid, and then stuck his finger in through the hole.

'Where's your finger, Mama? Put it through the hole,' he said. Taylor, terrified not to comply, manoeuvred her tied up hands through the limited space, up across her body to the hole. He removed his finger and she stuck one of hers up through the hole, the middle finger.

'Keep your finger there, Mama, so that I know you are there and that you love me.' He lay down on the floor next to the finger popping out through the hole. He caressed the finger, much to Taylor's disgust. She tried to withdraw it but he grabbed it and held on while he continued to caress and circle the top with the fingers of his other hand.

'Sing me a lullaby, Mama!' he insisted. This was getting more disturbing by the second but Taylor complied with the only lullaby she knew.

'Hush little baby, don't say a word...' she sang, creeping herself out, as he continued to lie in a foetal position next to the hole, sucking his thumb, and stroking her finger for hours.

He then remembered to feed her and give her water. He addressed her differently than at breakfast, kinder, more compassionate. He called her Mama the whole time.

Then he sealed her up under the floor and left her there for five hours until he considered it suppertime.

This meal was fed to her in morsels through the hole. There was no sitting up. He gave her a warning to open her mouth and poured water through the hole. It splashed all over her face, ran down her neck and soaked her shirt.

Charles Rose then opened the lower lid and ripped off her nappy, violently. The adhesive tape twisted in restraint and cut into her skin before snapping. He raped her, and then aggressively applied a fresh nappy without cleaning her.

She cried loudly throughout most of the night. She thought it might make him feel sympathetic if he heard her but instead every time she cried he jerked himself off. She tried to stop herself from crying but the more she tried to stop the more uncontrollable her sobbing became, and the louder the bed creaked above her, and the louder he groaned in pleasure. So she purposely did a poo so that he would have to deal with that at breakfast. But then she had to lie in it all night.

By morning, she seriously regretted it but through the hole she asked for breakfast before being changed. He complied, and went off to make her a fried egg sandwich with freshly squeezed orange juice.

It felt so good to sit up even if she was sitting in her own shit. The juice was so refreshing. He handfed her, and she chewed ravenously.

She started to feel so ashamed about the stinky mess she was sitting in and she tried to stall him changing her. She started a conversation with him.

'So do you live in his house all alone?'

'Yup!' he replied curtly.

'Lived here long?'

'All my life. My grandfather built it,' he told her in short to the point replies, putting paste on her toothbrush.

'Did he build the torture chamber you have me locked in?'

'Yup!'

'Don't they call what you've got on your lip a hair lip? Why do they call it that? Is it supposed to be hairy? Yours isn't hairy!'

'No, it is not a harelip which is called that because the cleft is like on a hare between the top lip and the bunny's nose. It is not a cleft palate either which means the roof of the mouth has not fused. No, this lip was given to me by a diamond ring my father wore which he inherited from his father, along with this house. Any more questions?' he informed her, speaking abruptly.

'Yes. Why are you doing this to me?'

'For three reasons: one, to keep me company. Two, you are an experiment for me to be able to determine how long my mother would have lived if my father hadn't snapped her neck when he punched her in the face repeatedly as he raped her. And thirdly, to make you a more appreciative person, and so you will grow into more deserving woman,' he told her. 'Now lie down, and keep your mouth shut or I will put duct tape over it again.'

She lay down obediently. She knew what was coming next.

'I'm sorry about the mess,' she said, as he was closing the top lid. She said it almost apologetically. It was not him she felt sorry for but herself. She was apologising to herself for the humiliation the next few minutes would be.

He opened the bottom lid and removed her nappy, said nothing and wiped her clean with baby wet wipes as if he was used to it, and it was something he had done often. That was a scary thought.

He applied the cream sexually this time. Not once did he call her Mama. Not until he came inside her and screamed out, 'OH MAMA!'

Taylor wondered how twisted this man's childhood could have been.

After that, Charles Rose put a fresh nappy on her, closed and locked the lid, dragged the bed over the doors, and went out for the entire day.

Taylor tried for hours to smash out the side of the box with her elbow. She was in so much agony when she gave up.

She began to concentrate, and tried to break the lid with her fingertips, but by trying to use her elbow to break the side of the box, she had damaged her arm too much to continue lifting it.

Taylor Mason actually survived under the floor for another three and a half months. By that time, she was wasting away, covered in sores and her body wouldn't let her sit up anymore for breakfast. Having to lie flat in such a small space for hours and hours, day after day was having a rapidly deteriorating affect on her body.

Mama had lasted two years under the floor but there were weeks in between that his father had let their mother up to resume her motherly duties like nothing out of the ordinary had been going on.

After a week or two, Philip Rose would find an excuse to put Nancy back down there. He would back up his actions with wicked lies that he would tell to the children of their mother's adulterous affairs, and how she was a bad mother who was planning to run away and leave them.

Charles Rose buried Taylor Morgan's body in the flowerbed of the small garden, and then went out for a drive to find her replacement.

It was months before he found a girl that was similar to how his mother had been when she was young; before his mother had met Philip Rose, her killer.

On a rainy afternoon in November of 1960, Charles Rose offered a lift to a girl standing in the rain waiting for a bus. Her hair was wet and dripping. He offered to drop her off at the next bus stop that had a shelter.

Hilary Haydon thought that as he would not be taking her far, just to the next stop, it would be fine. It was too far and unsafe to walk along the dark wet streets in that downpour, and it would save her money on the bus too. She agreed and got into his car.

'There's the next stop over there on the left,' she informed him, staring intently through the lashing rain. He injected the double dose of sedative into her neck before she could stop him.

Her face full of fear, she struggled to open the car door. He held onto her, put his foot on the accelerator, and drove past the bus stop at ninety miles per hour.

She started to drift away. She couldn't fight him. She slumped down against the window, like a tired girl taking a nap. He let go of her, relaxed his foot on the peddle, and drove calmly home.

When Hilary Haydon woke up she was in a dark box with her hands and feet bound. She began to have a panic attack, and she became so hysterical with fear that she passed out.

When she awoke, she could see light around her legs and a creepy man was putting a nappy on her. She whimpered. He closed the lid when he was done.

She slid up the box and put her eye to the hole. He saw the eyeball in the floor and it infuriated him. Her eyes were the wrong colour and her public hair had been blonde. The rain had darkened her hair but she was in fact fair-haired with green eyes. She was all wrong.

Charles Rose tried to stamp on the eyeball in fury. Hilary quickly turned her head to the side as his heavy boot stomped down over the hole.

He pulled the bed back over the doors, and left the house. Hilary Haydon screamed under the duct tape as loud as she could, which wasn't very loud and gave her an intense headache. She pounded on the lid with her bound fists. She banged on the sides of the box with her heels.

No one heard her.

Charles Rose paid in cash for the strong acid used to eat through anything to unblock industrial drains, and then he returned home.

'Cou-ieee!' he called. Hilary put her eye to the hole to see what was going on. It was the last thing she would ever see. Charles Rose poured the industrial acid through the hole into her eyes and all over her face.

Hilary Haydon only lived six more hours. Charles Rose buried Hilary's partially faceless body in the flower bed next to Taylor Mason.

Charles Rose met his third and last victim, Susan Rockton, one whole year before he met the love of his life, Ana Baxter, who would soon become Mrs. Charles Rose.

# CHAPTER EIGHT

Charles Rose found Susan Rockton just three days after he buried Hilary Haydon.

A year later, soon after meeting the stunning red head, Ana Baxter, who looked nothing like his mother, Charles Rose started to allow Susan Rockton to get out of the box twice a week to have a shower so that her stink would not seep up through the floorboards on the rare occasion that his new red-headed girlfriend came over.

Dark haired blue eyed Susan Rockton was a prostitute that Charles Rose had found wandering the streets. He would not usually be attracted to dirty whores but she looked more like his mother than anyone he had ever met, and his father told him repeatedly that his mother was a dirty whore so Susan Rockton seemed very appropriate. He invited the dark-haired blue-eyed junkie into his car.

The first few weeks had been worse for Susan as she had to go through withdrawal down there in that restricted space. He had kept her hydrated and she survived the two weeks of absolute hell. But in the end, she was the most changed, the most grateful, and she survived the longest.

In the sixth month of their relationship, mostly spent at her house, Ana Baxter found out that she was two months pregnant and that it was going to be a boy.

Charles Rose was overjoyed at the prospect of having a son. It was time for a new life.

Charles Rose knew he had to change his ways, and empty the box under the floor.

The garden was too small to fit another body in it so he decided to leave her in the box.

One afternoon out of the blue, fast setting concrete started pouring in through the hole.

At first Susan screamed.

As it hardened, it began to compress and shatter her ribs and other bones. She drowned painfully, as the box slowly filled up over her face.

Charles Rose sealed up the hole in the floor and the locks, blending them in perfectly with the wood. Then he laid lino, and then a thick fluffy white carpet on top of that, telling his pregnant girlfriend that the wood floor was getting damaged. He insisted that they should sell both their houses, and buy somewhere better for the baby to grow up, and he would get a better price if he kept the floors protected, hence having invested in the carpeting.

Even through the concrete and the carpeting, Susan Rockton was wafting a faint odour that to his paranoia was becoming more and more noticeable. Charles Rose was quick to find his new family a new house.

Four devastating years of marriage later, the son of Charles Rose and his wife, Ana Rose, disappeared on a cold winter morning. His father had sent him to his room after the three year-old boy had said "Bugger" at the breakfast table.

An hour later, his mother had gone to check on him and found that he was not in his room. His mother was worried that he had gone out to play without his coat on which still hung on the back of the kitchen chair.

Three weeks later, her son was found by the police in a box, placed in a shallow grave in the ground behind their house. Charles Rose was found guilty and confessed. He was sentenced to be hanged at Strangeways Prison on the 13th of August, 1964.

His wife did not go to watch.

# CHAPTER NINE

In 1977, Delwyn Mundy had been laid off from his higher paying job as chief of staff at the shopping precinct. This was very bad timing as his wife, Carrie, had just had a baby six months before.

Luckily, through persistent interviewing he was able to get himself a new job selling internet advertising which also meant he could work from home to help raise their daughter, Hayley.

The new job did not pay as much as they were used to, so they would have to downsize the mortgage payments.

Delwyn and Carrie sold the larger house, and bought a one story house on Culloden Hill Drive. It was an old property which had been on the market a long time. It really needed revamping in every room and lots of tender loving care but Carrie was up for the challenge. Best of all there was a little garden for Hayley to play in.

Hayley was eight months old by the time the sale of the two houses had gone through and they finally moved into the new house.

They could not afford decorators so they would have to do it themselves bit by bit. Delwyn promised to devote three hours in between work each day to help Carrie.

For the first year, Hayley had been a marvellous baby. In the beginning she was content to sit in her highchair with a snack and watch her mother strip and paint the walls.

Carrie started with the kitchen that faced the green with the park across the road. This would be handy for when Hayley was older and went to play in the park with her friends. Carrie could keep an eye on her.

Carrie painted the kitchen in a happy sunny yellow with a white backsplash around the cooker and sink. By the time she had completed the hall, the spare bedroom, the bathroom, the living room, and had moved onto the master bedroom at the back of the house, Hayley was already walking.

Hayley always acted unusually whenever she entered their bedroom and was put down onto the floor. She would always toddle to the end of the bed and then lie down on the floor in the child pose - her check against the floorboards, her legs bent underneath her with her nappy bottom up in the air.

'Mama,' Hayley suddenly said. Carrie was thrilled as it had been Hayley's first word but it was strange how Hayley had not been looking at her when she said it. It was almost like she had been listening to the floor and had heard her Mama. It was a little creepy.

Carrie shook off her negativity, and swooped up her daughter to kiss and praise her. Hayley giggled.

Carrie rushed into the spared bedroom that was being used by Delwyn as a study.

'Hayley said Mama! It was really clear!' Carrie told her husband, delighted.

'Awww cute! Who's a clever girl then!' he said, standing up to tickle and kiss his daughter who giggled. 'Can you say Daddy?'

'Give her a chance! She needs time to savour her first word,' Carrie said, smirking. Her husband laughed and tickled her too. Mother and daughter squirmed and giggled.

'Quick, let's go before Daddy tickles us to death!' Carrie teased, and ran off with Hayley.

'I will come help you strip the wallpaper off the back bedroom in ten minutes. I'm nearly finished,' Delwyn called after her.

'Okay, I'll make a cup of tea for the workers, and get Hayley settled,' she called back. She went to the kitchen and placed Hayley in her highchair and gave her a Rusk to suck on.

'Here, drink this, and then let's get cracking on the stripping,' Carrie encouraged, handing him a cup of tea.

'Sounds like the good old days!' he teased.

'Cheeky! But things are still good, aren't they?' Carrie asked.

'Of course they are! They are just different now that we have so much going on and we are so exhausted,' he replied. 'But I'm sure we will get our mojo back when we have finished the house.'

'And Emily goes to nursery, and moves into her own bedroom, and I lose this tire around my waist and regain my confidence,' Carrie added. Delwyn sighed but said nothing.

'Shall we get on with it then?' prompted Carrie. He followed her to the kitchen where they dumped their cups by the sink. Carrie scooped up Hayley who was holding her second Rusk and carried her to the bedroom. Delwyn followed.

They stopped in the doorway. The bed had moved ten centimetres away from the wall.

# CHAPTER TEN

'Did you move the bed?' Delwyn asked his wife, hoping she would say yes.

'I was waiting for you to do it,' she replied with a tone he had been dreading. Lately, Carrie had complained of hearing strange things in the house: footsteps, scratching, banging and crying. Delwyn wanted to dismiss it but he too thought he had heard faint screaming one night.

'Let's just get on with it. If you give these things attention you give them energy, so just ignore it. That is the best thing to do,' Delwyn told her.

Carrie put Hayley down on the floor.

'Watch her for a second while I go and get her play pen,' Carrie said to her husband, and left to go get the pen from the living room so that Hayley could play safely while they worked.

When she returned, Delwyn looked pale. He was looking down at the floor by his feet. Carrie entered the room and walked around the bed to see what he was looking at. Hayley was on the floor at his feet with her bum up in the air, her ear pressed against the floor, looking under the bed.

'Mama,' she was repeating. Delwyn had wanted to pick her up and congratulate her when he first heard it but when he looked and saw that she was facing under the bed while she said it, he felt something was not right about it.

The legs and curled feet of the bed were carved into the ornate sideboards which in design rose and fell like decorative wooden curtains, allowing only a peek into the darkness under the heavy antique bed. Delwyn didn't want to get close and look under the bed.

All of a sudden the baby started scratching frantically at the floor.

'Mama,' she said again. It was chilling, and so was the dramatic drop in temperature.

'What do you think she is doing?' Carrie asked him, perturbed.

'I don't know but something under the bed or under the floor she is relating to you. Did you put something under the bed?'

'No! Why would I?' she retorted, crossly. Carrie was shivering.

'Put her in her pen before she hurts herself and ruins the floor,' Delwyn told her. He picked Hayley up and passed her to her mother who put her in the pen with her soft toys. Then Carrie went to get a small heater to warm up the room.

The two adults got to work, stripping off all the dirty white wallpaper. Carrie was satisfyingly pulling off a really large strip when scratches started to appear on the wall beneath. Carrie screamed and let go of the paper. Delwyn turned. Carrie lifted the paper again. The scratches were letters, almost a completed and predictable word that was continuing to carve itself into the plaster on wall.

'Okay, don't give it any energy. Take Hayley in the living room for ten minutes. I'll get some of that sage we have in the kitchen,' Delwyn instructed.

'At least that crappy ghosting hunting documentary we watched turned out to be useful for something,' Carrie said, grabbing Hayley and vacating the room.

'It was sage they burnt wasn't it? Carrie?'

'Yes! Burn the whole lot! Get whatever that was out of here, or I am not going in that bedroom again! Hayley and I will sleep in the spare room. See how fast you get your mojo on then! I mean it! Get rid of it, Delwyn!' came Carrie's hysterical reply from the living room where she was putting on cartoons for Hayley.

'I'm trying! Calm down or you are just feeding it energy.'

'Just what I needed to hear!' Carrie retorted, sarcastically. She needed to calm down for Hayley not to feel alarmed.

She crossed her legs on the sofa next to Hayley who was lying on her belly watching a bright coloured animation with horse characters. Carrie closed her eyes and began to focus, surrounding her and Hayley in a circle of projected white light to protect them. She focused on her breathing, in through the nose for four counts, exhaling out through the mouth for eight counts. She focused on Delwyn burning the sage in their bedroom and surrounded him in a circle of white light. She breathed in through the nose and exhaled through her mouth.

Where was Hayley?

Most mothers can feel the presence of their child even in another room. Hayley's presence was gone. Carrie's eyes shot open. She screamed.

Delwyn, carrying a smoking bunch of sage, ran into the room that his wife was ransacking in a frantic search for her missing eleven-month-old.

'I can't find her, Delwyn! She was right next to me on the sofa! I was meditating beside her and I suddenly felt she was gone.'

'Don't panic! She is here somewhere! She might have toddled off into another room,' he said going out into the hall. He looked in the bathroom, the kitchen, in the spare bedroom, under his desk, in the cupboards, under cushions, amongst the toys, in the bath, and even down the toilet.

# CHAPTER ELEVEN

Carrie rushed to the master bedroom; ugly with its half torn paper cast in shadow by the rainclouds gathering over the small fenced in garden outside the bay window.

She listened for her child. She could hear something scratching. Where was it coming from? She walked around the bed to the window to see if the noise was coming from outside. No, it was definitely inside the room.

She got down on her knees and peeked through the gap carved in the mahogany shirt around the antique bed. She felt it was not a good space, it felt chilling, but could see only blackness. It gave her the creeps so she quickly got up. Hayley could not have fit through the gaps in the sideboards of the bed anyway and she wondered why she had been drawn to look under there.

'Hayley? Where are you, baby? Come to Mummy,' Carrie called, looking in a pile of washing, in cupboards, and under all the clothes hanging in the closet.

The scratching started again. It wasn't a slow clawing, it was more like someone was carving through the wood with something like a pencil or a small screwdriver or a knife or a nail. Carrie stopped to listen.

'Mama,' Carrie heard Hayley's baby voice say. She didn't sound afraid; she sounded like she could see her mother. Where was she? Carrie looked around frustrated and afraid.

'Hayley, where are you, baby? I'm here baby. Come here, Hayley, where Mummy can see you. Come here, baby.' There was no reply but the scratching sounded again. She listened at the wall but it seemed like it was coming from the centre of the room behind her.

With strain and effort, Carrie pushed the bed back against the wall. She stood at the end of it and looked down at the floor. She traced over the wooden planks with her bare foot. There was something there. Something felt different; a small circular patch where the wood seemed fake. It was filled in with wood filler or something and then skilfully painted over to blend in with the rest of the wooden floor. Carrie got down on the knees and scraped at it with her finger. Then she got up and went to the closet.

On tip toes, she reached up for the knife that Delwyn hid on the shelf at the top of the closet under his fluffy jumpers. It was there for protection in an extreme case of someone breaking into the house to rape and kill his family.

Carrie dug out the circular patch in the floor with the knife.

'Why the fuck are you digging holes in the floor while I am frantically trying to find our lost child?' Delwyn demanded.

'She is here, somewhere! She said, "Mama". I heard her!'

'And you think somehow she managed to get under the floorboards?' Delwyn said, pulling her up from the floor and giving his

84

worried wife a needed hug. 'Did you find anything?'

'Only concrete,' Carrie sobbed onto his shoulder.

'We will find her,' Delwyn promised his wife. 'You check every room again. I am going to check the garden and outside in the street. If we don't find her, then I think we might need to call the police.' She nodded on his shoulder, sniffed and pulled away.

Carrie went to search the other rooms again. Delwyn searched the garden and the street. When he got back, his wife was in the back bedroom and had torn up a whole floor board, only to reveal more concrete, but she had her cheek pressed against it, listening to it.

'What are you doing?'

'SSSSHHHHhhh!' she shushed him, holding her hand up to silence him. 'Listen!'

He listened but could hear nothing. Just as he was about to speak, the scratching sound started again, continuously for a whole minute. He got closer to the end of the bed, conscious that his ankles were close to the gap in the ornate frame of the hideous old bed that exposed the blackness beneath.

He got down on his hands and knees with his wife, and listened to the concrete. They heard eerie heavy breathing. Someone was under their floor.

'Mama,' said Hayley's voice behind them, making them both jump out of their skins. Hayley toddled over to her relieved parents who smothered their giggling child in kisses.

# CHAPTER TWELVE

Delwyn nailed the floorboard back into place but had no wood filler for the hole so that would have to wait until his next visit to the DIY shop. He planned to go on the Wednesday to pick up the magnolia paint for both bedrooms.

They bought and burnt plenty of sage. They made holy water with lots of sea salt and by saying blessings and prayers for the house over it, before they flung droplets all over the walls and clothes and bed and furniture, saying over and over that they wished the spirits to leave.

The three of them slept close together with Hayley in the middle.

The next day, Carrie sighed heavily when the holy water had dried. There were saltwater stains over all her clothes and the furniture. So she had to wipe everything down.

'Good thing we didn't paint the walls yet or we would have had to paint them again,' she yelled to Delwyn who was working in his office. 'Bloody saltwater stained everything! I have to clean all the windows again and wipe everything, and I mean everything!'

'Babe, I'm working! I can't deal with it now! Can you see to whatever it is? I'll help you later!' he called back. Hayley was having a nap in her playpen in the living room so Carrie just got on with it.

She was wiping the floor with a cloth, when someone invisible grabbed her and threw her on her back and started punching her violently in the face. The blows kept coming and she did not have time to breath or scream.

Delwyn did not see her as he walked out of his office which was the room next to the one in which his wife was silently being beaten to pulp.

From the floor behind the bed, she saw her husband pass by the doorway as she looked up for help. She tried to scream but nothing came out, and her attempt was silenced with another left hook from a powerful invisible fist. A tooth flew out of her mouth and through the gap of the ornate mahogany skirt into the darkness underneath the bed. Her face ricocheted.

Then she felt like she was dropped. Her head and shoulders collapsed onto the floor.

She felt like she had an invisible strip of masking tape stuck over her mouth. She sensed something like an invisible lid close above her.

Someone was touching her legs, and then pulling down her painting shorts. She screamed and struggled but she was restrained by the invisible lid above her head. It felt like she was in a long box. She would come to describe the feeling as an invisible coffin above ground.

She struggled to hold her shorts up but then the invisible someone bound her hands with what felt like cable ties. He didn't remove the shorts in the end but despite having her clothes still on she felt him penetrate her. He violently raped her. It was extremely painful. Carrie's screaming and loud sobbing were muffled by the duct tape.

Delwyn caught sight of his wife's legs in the air when he passed back with his snack. He entered the room to see what she was up to. The scene disturbed him more than anything else he had ever seen in his life. His wife had her head and shoulders on the floor, her hands were held together and she was pushing or pounding on invisible glass or something straight and solid like an invisible door, exactly four centimetres above her chest.

He could see she wasn't faking it as a joke because this peculiar movement was precise every time. It looked extremely uncomfortable, and his wife's smashed up, contorted and bleeding face was a sordid picture of blood vessel bursting strain and fury.

However, as he came more around the bed, the most unbelievable and shocking part of her body came into view. Her lower back and bottom and legs were suspended in the air. Delwyn might have presumed that his wife had been practising yoga on the sly for her whole life had it not for the violent jerking and thrusts. She was moving like there was no gravity, like someone was holding legs up. Like someone was fucking her. Like someone was raping her.

Delwyn ran around the bed and tried to grab his battered wife but his hands met an invisible door above her. She scratched at it frantically, her eyes pleading him to save her. He tried to grab her bent up jerking legs but some invisible force pushed him violently away. He flew across the room and hit the wall.

'GET OUT!' raged Delwyn, running at the invisible man with full speed and full force.

Carrie's legs instantly fell to the floor with a thud. Whoever it was had gone. Carrie was able to sit up and kiss her hero who then held her as she sobbed for a long time.

# CHAPTER THIRTEEN

'We need to get out of here, Delly! All of us. Now!' Carrie insisted.

'Where would we go Carrie? Every penny we have goes into paying for this house. We have no spare cash for a hotel or even a cheap motel. We have no family or friends that could put us up long term. We can't go anywhere, Carrie!' he said bluntly, stroking her head. 'I am sorry but we are stuck here. We will just have to hope it goes away if we don't give it any energy, and we just keep cleansing the house all the time.'

'I don't think it is safe for Hayley at the moment. Tania from the Mother and Baby group has a spare bedroom. I'm going to give her a call and see if we can spend the weekend there,' Carrie told him, wiping her face, and standing up.

Carrie went to the living room to check on Hayley who was still sleeping soundly in her pen with her stuffed animals scattered about her. Carrie turned her back for an instant to pick up the phone and dial Tania's number; then turned back to look at her beautiful sleeping angel.

The toys were arranged around her child in a rectangular shape. Her baby was a ghastly shade of blue. Carrie ran to the crib. She checked to feel Hayley's breathing on her cheek. Nothing! She checked for a pulse. Nothing!

'Hello? Hello? Anyone there? Carrie is that you? Can you hear me?' said Tania's voice from the phone. Carrie rushed back to the phone, pressed the button to cut Tania off, and called for an ambulance.

'Emergency services, how can I help you?'

'Ambulance! I need an ambulance! My eleven-month-old was sleeping and now she is blue and not breathing.'

'Okay. Are you the mother?'

'Yes, I just said my eleven-month-old, didn't I?'

'Okay keep calm, can you tell me your full name and address please.'

'Carrie Louise Mundy. Twelve Culloden Hill Drive, Essex. Please hurry!'

'The ambulance is on the way, Carrie. My name is Sarah and I have three kids, and I'm going to talk you through this. Okay? Now I need you to tilt your child's head up, and check the throat for anything blocking the airway. First look, and then feel with your fingers gently down the throat. Is this your son or daughter?'

'Daughter,' Carrie informed her, opening Hayley's mouth and looking and feeling down her throat. 'There's nothing!'

'What is your daughter's name?'

'Hayley.'

'Okay, I want you to place two fingers in the middle of Hayley's breastbone just below the nipple line, and you are going to push down almost four centimetres. Each time you give a compression, allow the chest to rise before doing it again. Do this thirty times and then tilt her head back by using one hand on the forehead and two fingers under the chin. Cover her nose and mouth with your mouth and give two slow small breathes making sure her chest rises between each breath. Then give thirty more compressions with your two fingers and then two breaths. Continue this until you see signs of life or until the ambulance crew arrive to take over. I will stay on the line until they get there. Place the phone on the floor beside you. Count out loud so that I can hear you.'

Carrie could hear the ambulance siren a few streets away. She ceaselessly continued to give compressions but the panic was building in her throat and chest, threatening to choke her.

'She is not responding!' Carrie cried.

'Keep going, Carrie, you are doing very well. The ambulance is close by.'

'I can hear them. Please tell them to hurry!'

'They are almost there, Carrie. Keep going.'

The paramedics came running in when a surprised Delwyn opened the door to their persistent banging. When they asked where his daughter was, Delwyn turned deathly pale, pointed to the bedroom at the back and then ran ahead of them.

He found Carrie with Hayley on the floor. Hayley was a horrible shade of grey.

The paramedics told them to step back. They put adhesive defibrillator pads on Hayley's chest. The battery powered machine sent electric shocks through her heart. Surprisingly, Hayley coughed back to life with the first jolt.

Carrie wept with relief. She sobbed in Delwyn's arms as a paramedic picked Hayley up and carried her to the ambulance.

Hayley was kept in the hospital overnight for observation. Carrie stayed with her and slept uncomfortably in the chair in her room. There was not room for both parents to stay so Delwyn went home alone, feeling shaken but thankful.

He went straight to the back bedroom, kicked off his shoes and lay exhausted on the old antique bed. The house seemed deathly quiet without his wife and child there - until the scratching began.

Delwyn sat up and looked over the edge of the bed. He gazed at the hole in the floor.

'Is that you, Charlie?' he heard a woman's voice say, and an eyeball appeared in the hole.

Horrified, Delwyn leapt back across the bed. He started sweating profusely, his heart banging in his chest, his breaths shallow.

He calmed himself. What he had seen was impossible. He crawled to the end of the bed and looked down at the hole. There was nothing there. Maybe he had imagined it because he was so tired. He got off the bed and walked around and knelt on the floor. With trepidation, he put his finger in the hole. As expected, he felt only concrete below. He obviously needed sleep. He thought the stress of almost losing his child must be playing tricks on his weary mind.

He returned to the bed and lay down. Within minutes he was snoring.

The temperature in the room dropped dramatically. Delwyn's exhaled breathes became visible like fog, as the wretched spirit of Susan Rockton crawled into the bed beside him.

# CHAPTER FOURTEEN

In the morning, Delwyn collected his wife and child from the hospital in their orange Volvo hatchback.

The doctors had said Hayley might have died momentarily of cot death. They advised her parents to keep a close eye on her at home and to remove all pillows, blankets and toys from her crib.

Carrie and Delwyn stared obsessively at their daughter all day, and half of the night but she seemed fine and was breathing quite normally in the crib beside their bed. Exhausted, they both eventually fell asleep.

Carrie was awoken by the sound of scratching. Hayley was not in her crib. She wasn't able to get out of it alone; someone would have to lift her out. Carrie shot a look behind her but Delwyn was sound asleep.

Carrie heard the scratching again coming from below the foot of the bed. She jumped up and ran round the bed. There was Hayley manically scratching at the floorboards, her little baby fingers all bloody. Carrie scooped her up and rushed her to their bedroom sink to run her hands under the water. Carrie had always thought it strange to have a sink in their bedroom but now she was glad of it.

She bandaged Hayley's damaged fingers, and took her child back into the bed with her to keep her safe. The odd thing was, Hayley had not cried at all and her fingers must have hurt a lot but she had continued to use them to scrape away at the wood floor, demonically.

Why did Hayley always scratch at the same place by the foot of the bed? Carrie knew there was something there, and even if it took a sledge hammer, she was determined to get to the bottom of it.

The next day was a beautiful sunny Saturday, and they spent most of it as a family in the garden. Carrie had made freshly squeezed lemonade. The adults were enjoying a respite from gardening in the shade of the apple tree. Hayley was digging in the flowerbed with her plastic trowel. She seemed excited and was yelling, 'Mama! Mama! Mama!' Carrie laughed.

'What baby? Do you love gardening?' Carrie cooed. She turned to her husband and

told him that they might have a green fingered
child.

'She takes after you then...No! Hayley,
don't get your bandages dirty!' Dewlyn said,
distracted by his daughter who had ditched the
trowel and was now digging frantically at the
earth like a dog.

'Mama! Mama! Mama!' cried Hayley,
going ballistic and digging deeper, soil flying
in all directions. Carrie went over to retrieve
her child who kicked and screamed as her
mother carried her into the house to change her
bandages. Delwyn went with them to see if he
could help calm her.

'Mama! Mama! Mama!' Hayley continued
to scream.

'When are you going to say Daddy? Say Daddy! Daddy,' Delwyn encouraged, trying to distract his daughter as her mother sat her on the kitchen counter, holding her with one hand and reaching for the first aid box with the other.

'Daddy, say Daddy,' he tried again.

'Cunt!' said a demonic voice that came from his eleven-month-old baby girl's mouth.

Carrie and Delwyn both looked at their child in shock, and then looked at each other to confirm that they had both heard it. Neither of them spoke, and Hayley remained quiet but as if unaware that anything unusual had happened. Bewildered and in shock, Carrie washed and bandaged Hayley's hands.

'I'm calling Tania!' Carrie stated when she had finished. 'I have to get Hayley out of this house!'

# CHAPTER FIFTEEN

Tania had agreed to let all three of them stay the weekend in her spare bedroom. They had arrived grateful that afternoon. However, from the moment that Tania had greeted them with a smile at her front door, Hayley had started kicking off.

'Mama! Mama! Mama!' Hayley screamed over and over, all afternoon, all evening, and all night. She had kept the whole household awake. It didn't matter that Carrie held her and told her that she was there. Hayley did not stop when Carrie sang to her and tried to sooth her. Over and over and over, Hayley continued to scream for her Mama.

Tania was trying to be an understanding host but Carrie and Delwyn knew they could not continue to put Tania's family through that.

After breakfast, Carrie hugged her friend and thanked her but said that they were going to leave. Tania said it was a shame but she was silently relieved, as were her tired husband her two seven-year-old twins.

They drove in their orange Volvo to the clinic. Carrie tried to explain the situation to the receptionist, and then sat waiting to be seen by the paediatrician.

Hayley continued to scream for her mama as the doctor looked her over. He ran a few tests but could not find anything medically wrong with her. He looked at her hands and

Carrie explained how she had scratched on the floor wearing away at the skin around her nails and tops of her fingers.

The doctor sent them home with the advice to give Hayley Calpol to calm her, and to keep a close eye on her.

There was nowhere else they could go so they followed the doctor's advice and went home. From the moment they walked through their front door, Hayley ceased her non-stop screaming.

Carrie placed Hayley in her highchair and gave her a Rusk to suck on so she could make herself a well-deserved cup of tea. Delwyn had gone back to work in the spare room office.

It had started to rain heavily. Carrie was drawn to the window by a loud clap of thunder. Lightning struck the pavement outside the house.

In the place where the lightning had struck now stood a pale figure. It was a girl of about seventeen. She was drenched from the rain but she stayed on the pavement, looking at Carrie. She looked cold and dishevelled, helpless and scared. She was saying something but Carrie could not hear her.

Carrie rushed to the door to see if the girl needed help.

'Are you okay?' Carrie called from the doorway.

'TELL HIM I'M BLONDE! DON'T LET HIM TAKE ME! TELL HIM I AM

BLONDE!' shouted the girl through the rain from where she stood on the pavement. Carrie didn't understand but she could see the teenager was in distress.

'Do you want to come inside? I can make you a cup of tea and get you a towel,' Carrie offered. Suddenly the girl was behind her in the hallway. Carrie jumped.

'GET ME OUT!' screamed the girl in Carrie's face, and then she vanished.

Carrie ran screaming down the hallway to Delwyn's office. She burst through the door, startling him, and explained what had happened.

'Where's Hayley?' he replied in panic.

'She's in the kitchen,' Carrie told him. She rushed back to check on her daughter but Hayley was gone.

They both searched the house in frantic panic. Through the back bedroom window, Carrie caught sight of her baby outside in the rain, digging in the muddy flowerbed. Carrie opened the back door that led from the bedroom to the garden and hurried over to her child. What she saw made her reel back in disgust. Hayley was kissing a decayed human skull and calling it, 'Hilary'.

# CHAPTER SIXTEEN

Six days after the police dug up the entire garden, the three bodies that had been found in the flowerbed where identified to be a teenage girl called Hilary Haydon who went missing in November of 1960, Taylor Mason who went missing in March of 1960, and Nancy Rose who had once lived in the house with her husband Philip and their three children, Harry, Judy, and Charles.

For weeks, reporters were knocking on their door trying to get an interview with the couple who lived in the house of horror on Culloden Hill Drive. They allowed themselves to be photographed and said a few words about being glad it was all over, hoping that the reporters would then go away and leave them in peace. Newspapers featured front page articles on what they had managed to dig up on the odd Rose family, focusing mostly on Charles Rose who had been hung for murdering his son, and was presumably responsible for the murder of his mother and the teenagers, Hilary Haydon and Taylor Mason.

Carrie and Delwyn were not pleased to find out the gruesome details that were known about the history of their house but they hoped now that the spirits would be laid to rest and the haunting would stop.

After a few months everything settled down, and they were living contently without complaint in the house.

Hayley started to go once a week to a toddlers nursery. She made some friends her age and enjoyed the finger painting and story time.

One morning, Hayley was playing in the sandpit with Marcus and Melinda who were both two-years-old. Hayley emptied the wooden box of all the buckets and spades, and had told Melinda to get inside. Melinda was a waif of a child and fit easily into the small box. Hayley dug a deep hole in the sandpit and Marcus helped her.

Then Hayley put the lid on the box, and got Marcus to help her push it into the hole which they then covered up with sand, burying their friend inside.

At the last minute, their teacher realised that both Melinda and the toy box were missing. She rushed over and asked Marcus and Hayley if they had seen where Melinda went to. They both pointed to the sand. The teacher dug furiously and pulled out the box to release Melinda. She was okay, just a bit shaken when she realised she was finding it hard to breathe.

The teacher called Carrie who came to pick Hayley up. Carrie lectured her toddler all the way home about the dangers of burying people. Hayley listened intently but remained quiet.

Delwyn was going to build a small shed in the garden that he could use as an office space so that Hayley could have his current office as her bedroom. Until he found the time to complete such a task, the three of them were sleeping together in the mahogany bed in the magnolia back bedroom.

At three-thirteen in the morning Delwyn awoke to the pressure of someone sitting on his chest. He opened his eyes to see a dark haired young woman staring into his face. He tried to cry out but was unable to make a sound as his mouth and nostrils were full of a hardening slush of cement. He couldn't breathe. Suffocating, he reached over and shook his wife awake. Carrie started screaming.

Hayley woke up too, and screamed, 'GO!' at the girl. The apparition disappeared and so

119

did the cement. Delwyn coughed and sputtered, deeply breathing oxygen into his lungs. Carrie comforted him, and got him a glass of water from the sink.

Hayley had climbed off the bed and was on the floor with ear to the wood.

'Not Mama! Not Mama!' she started saying over and over again. She stuck her little finger into the shallow hole. She then knocked on the floor and said, 'Hello?'

Delwyn and Carrie watched her from where they were both sat at the foot of the bed.

'Not Mama!' Hayley told them, pointing to the hole. She knocked on the wood again.

'Hello?'

GIRL UNDER THE FLOOR

Carrie screamed when the eyeball appeared in the hole, looking at her daughter. Delwyn snatched his child off the floor and passed her to her mother.

'That's it!' fumed Delwyn, storming out of the room to get his sledge hammer. He came back like a madman on a mission. Carrie took Hayley out of the room.

When the police arrived an hour later, responding to a noise complaint from their neighbours, Delwyn had smashed through the first layer of concrete, and the half decomposed corpse was starting to reveal itself.

Carrie showed the police officers into her bedroom where her sweating husband was smashing up the floor. There was a horrific stench of death.

The police officers told Delwyn to put the sledge hammer down and to step away. Back up and forensics were called in. Carrie and Delwyn were taken down to the station to be questioned.

When forensics had determined that the murder had taken place back in the sixties before Carrie and Delwyn had lived at the house, it was concluded that the crime had been committed by the same perpetrator who had murdered the women found in the flowerbeds. The body was identified as Susan Rockton aged nineteen.

As soon as they return from the police station, Delwyn phoned a realtor and put the house on the market.

Carrie poured lines of salt in front of the windows and doors, burnt sage twice a day, and threw holy water over everything.

The floor was repaired and new wooden planks were laid. It took two months for them to get an offer on the house but they snatched up the first price they were offered.

Nothing strange had happened during the time they had kept busy by packing up to move out, until their last night in the house.

Carrie had decided that as their lives were changing and everything was going to be new that she would change her look.

She had bought a very dark brown dye from the chemist and she covered every inch of her shoulder length blonde hair in it, and waited forty minutes.

When dried it really suited her and made her blue eyes pop. She was really happy with the results. Delwyn liked it too. Hayley on the other hand did not seem too happy about it.

'NOT MAMA!' Hayley shouted at Carrie.

Before bed, Carrie sorted the last of their things into boxes and taped them shut.

Delwyn loaded the Volvo with as much as possible and the rest was stacked by the front door for the removals van that was coming in the morning.

They closed their eyes that night with relief, and also excitement for the new chapter in their lives which would begin the next day. They were both glad to be shot of the house on Culloden Hill Drive and were looking forward to a new start.

Carrie drifted off into a peaceful sleep. When she awoke, her hands and ankles were bound with cable ties, her mouth was covered by duct tape, and she was lying in the darkness of a coffin shaped box.

When Delwyn awoke the next morning, his wife was gone. He searched for her, called the police, offered rewards and pleaded on national television for her to come home.

Carrie Louise Mundy was never found.

CPSIA information can be obtained
at www.ICGtesting.com
Printed in the USA
LVHW090754050821
694386LV00010B/551